0 0 NOV 2016

0 0 NOV 2016

Withdrawn

D0280017

Anancy & Friends

Cultural Folktales for Children

Beulah Richmond

LMH Publishing Limited

Cover Layout: Lee-Quee Designs

Edited by: Charles Moore / Mike Henry

Book Design, Layout & Typeset: PAGE Services

0 0 NOV 2016

Published by: LMH Publishing Limited
7 Norman Road,
LOJ Industrial Complex,
Building 10,
Kingston C.S.O., Jamaica.
Tel: 876-938-0005; 938-0712
Fax: 876-759-8752
Email: lmhbookpublishing@cwjamaica.com
Website: www.lmhpublishingjamaica.com

Printed in Jamaica by Smith's Printing Services Ltd.

ISBN: 976-8184-48-5

DEDICATION

To my granddaughter Yasmin,
who called forth the magic.

CONTENTS

THE GARDEN PATCH

Anancy, the spider, added the finishing touches to his home on the topmost branch of a tall tree towering above the other trees in the woods. Resting tiredly in his web, Anancy admired the wonderful view below, where the meadow stretched from the edge of the woods to a river in the distance. Brer Rabbit, Anancy's good friend, also lived in the woods and every evening when their daily work was done, these two would meet. Anancy, after spinning and mending his web, torn again and again by small birds and insects who got caught in it, would float on his silken thread to the tree's lowest branch.

There, he would await Brer Rabbit's return from a day

of weeding and planting carrots and turnips in his small garden patch. On a fallen log, both friends would sit and discuss the different problems that had befallen them the previous night and during the day.

As they talked, Brer Rabbit and Anancy stayed on the lookout for Sly Brer Fox, who would often creep up on them, sending Brer Rabbit into his hole and Anancy

2

hurriedly up his tree. Every evening as it got dark, Sly Brer Fox would move stealthily into Brer Rabbit's patch and steal most of his carrots and turnips. Brer Rabbit would set different traps, but Sly Brer Fox would always find them and laugh at his efforts. One night Anancy, seeing how frustrated and helpless his friend Brer Rabbit was, said, "Why don't we hatch a plan to catch Brer Fox?" And so Anancy came up with an idea: "Why not," he said, "make a look-alike Brer Rabbit out of wood and sticky glue and wrap a thick web around it?" And so, it was on one dreary night they put this fake Brer Rabbit in a very dark spot in the garden patch where only its outline could be seen.

That night, Sly Fox arrived with his bag slung over his back ready to pick the carrots and turnips. Looking across at the tree near the edge of the garden patch, he saw Brer Rabbit leaning against the trunk of a tree. Creeping silently towards Brer Rabbit, Sly Brer Fox thought how Brer Rabbit combined with the carrots and turnips would make a lovely stew for his dinner. Brer Fox smacked his lips in great anticipation as he leapt and grabbed Brer Rabbit's right ear, saying loudly, "Caught you at last, I am going to enjoy making a meal out of you. You, Brer Rabbit, have led me on a merry dance these long months. Now, no more!"

Suddenly, Sly Brer Fox realized that his right paw was stuck fast to Brer Rabbit's ear. Trying to free himself, he grabbed at the other ear with his left paw, now Brer Fox panicked and kicked with both feet. Realizing that he had been fooled by a made-up rabbit of paper, glue and a web, Brer Fox roared in anger; whereupon Anancy came down to see what all the yelling and noise was about. On seeing Sly Fox neatly snared, Anancy laughed in glee. Sly Fox pleaded with Anancy to go and get help to set him free, but Anancy only laughed louder and spun more webs around Sly Fox. He went off to tell Brer Rabbit.

Next morning, when Brer Rabbit and Anancy returned to the garden, Brer Fox begged and pleaded with them to free him, promising that he would never again steal Brer Rabbit's vegetables or disturb their nightly meetings.

Hoping that they could believe him and feeling that he had learned a lesson, Anancy and Brer Rabbit freed Brer Fox.

UNINVITED GUESTS

The following day, Anancy awoke feeling rested and refreshed from a good night's sleep. He sighed contentedly and thought, "Now that I have completed all my webs so cleverly hidden among the leaves and branches of my tree; and have trapped enough for a feast, I shall invite my good friend, Mia, over for dinner."

Mia, like many female spiders, did not like the outdoors, and so had made her home in an old abandoned shack deep in the woods. There, Mia found that she could spin her web safe from the wind and rain, and without those pesky creatures that had Anancy constantly spinning and mending his web.

Lately, though, Mia had acquired some pests of her own. The last time Anancy had dined with her, she had introduced him to Brer Mouse Marvin, who arrived on her doorstep on a cold and stormy night seeking shelter.

Marvin liked Mia's warm, cozy shack and had decided to stay and make it his home. With Marvin's arrival, Mia had to move her webs to the upper corners and into the ceiling because although Marvin moved about quietly

enough, his grandchildren, whenever they visited, were very
noisy and destructive, disturbing the peacefulness of the
shack. Two of them had even asked to stay, to which
Mia replied with a firm "No!"

Thinking now of Mia's troubles, little did Anancy realize
that his own worries were about to start.

Coming out of his web, Anancy saw in the distance,
by the river, some movement. Watching closely, he saw
Sly Brer Fox chasing a poor squirrel across the open field
towards the woods. Taking a closer look at the squirrel
as he neared the safety of the trees, Anancy realized that
it was Brer Theo, a troublesome 'brat' that Anancy had
had the misfortune to meet a few months ago.

Anancy watched as Theo reached the safety of the
woods and quickly darted up a tree. Disgusted with
himself for allowing a little squirrel to outrun him, Sly Brer
Fox, crouched beneath the tree in which Theo had taken

refuge and was now out of reach. Sly Fox sat and pondered his next move. Looking around he saw a large fowl coop on the other side of the woods. The last time Sly Fox had paid a visit there he had run into a little trouble, but as his tummy growled loudly he decided that he would risk another visit. And so, he waited until dark to venture out and hoped that the silly old hens would not cackle too loudly and have the man with the long gun come after him, again.

Up in his tree, Anancy watched as Sly Fox slunk off. With Sly Fox gone, Anancy saw Theo dart from his hiding place, looking carefully around to make sure that no other enemy was in sight. Then Theo did an odd thing: he kept climbing from one tree to the next as though looking for someone or something.

Forgetting Theo and his antics, Anancy went off to check his webs to see what they had caught overnight. This took Anancy all day as he had to extract each insect from the web and wrap it individually in a silken cocoon. That evening, after only a short meeting with his friend Brer Rabbit, Anancy retired early to bed, tired from a hard but very satisfying day's work.

Next morning, as Anancy opened his sleep-filled eyes, he looked straight into the eyes of none other than Theo. Startled, he scowled fiercely at the intruder who had dared to invade his home. "First, those pesky birds, and now Theo!" he thought.

"Good morning, Anancy, my good friend," said Theo with a grin on his mischievous face. "Yesterday, I looked all over for you, and last night I fell asleep in this lovely tree. After I got awake this morning, I came up here to

admire the view and, to my amazement, there you were asleep. I didn't wake you up, did I? I tried very hard to be ever so quiet, but you do have noisy birds living here. I think I will stay for a while and drive them away for you."

At the vision of Theo living here even for a short time, Anancy was horrified and speechless. But before Anancy could find his tongue, Theo had quickly darted off, taking his silence for consent.

A few days later, Anancy had Mia over for dinner. Relaxing after a very tasty meal, the two good friends sat talking about their latest troubles: how their once serene lives had changed since their last meeting. Mia mentioned that Marvin's grandchildren and his numerous relatives were making their visits much more often and staying for longer periods. She told Anancy that their noise and constant bickering were very upsetting and that she just had to find a way to get rid of Marvin and his family and get back to her former quiet and restful life.

Anancy, at the same time, talked to Mia about Theo and his troublesome habits. "Just imagine," Anancy said. "Two mornings ago, I went to my webs to collect the previous night's catch and what did I find in them? Nuts, of all things! And Theo had the audacity to tell me that he thought my webs an ideal place to store his nuts for the winter months, and after much trying I could get him to remove only a few nuts. And the promise he made to chase away the birds was never kept. Instead, he and the birds have become the best of friends."

Anancy and Mia talked until late in the night discussing different ways to get rid of their unwanted guests. As Mia got up to take her leave, Anancy said excitedly, "You know, Mia, I am sure our friend Brer Barney Owl can help us! And I think I will speak to him."

Barney, was a fierce-looking owl with bright and

glittering eyes who, on his nightly outings, would occasionally stop by Anancy's tree for a little chat. The next night, after only a short visit with Anancy, Barney flew off to pay a call on Mia, who was in her web hanging from the ceiling of her shack. Mia had given up any hope of sleeping as Marvin's grandchildren and relatives were having one of their usual noisy parties.

Suddenly, the door squeaked open and in came Theo with a bag filled with nuts over his shoulder. Theo, a cheeky smile on his face, looked at Marvin and his guests and said, "Hello, Marvin, nice party you are having. I will not disturb. I've just come over to pay a call on my good friend, Mia." Looking up at Mia in her web, Theo, with even a wider smile on his face, called out, "Hello, Mia, my friend. Anancy just told me of your very kind and wonderful offer to let me store a few of my nuts here

in some of your webs." Still smiling, Theo opened his bag of nuts.

In the silence that followed Theo's announcement, a loud and terrible hoot came from the open window, and in flew, Brer Barney, his great yellow eyes flashing fiercely. Fluttering his wings and glaring down at the frightened group below, he roared, "Woo-woo! Theo, you've been a nuisance to Anancy, and now you're about to be the same to Mia, storing your nuts in their webs. Brer Benjy, my friend the Hawk, is looking for a fat squirrel to feed his young family tonight. If you do not leave this part of the woods and never return, I will make sure that you end up as their next meal."

Shaking, Theo dropped his bag of nuts and raced through the door into the night. Hard on his heels followed Marvin and his family feeling that if they stayed around they might wind up as dessert for Brer Hawk. With peace and quiet restored, Barney gave Mia a big wink and flew off into the night.

The next night, when Brer Anancy and Mia met, there was much laughter and glee as they thought of the look on the faces of Theo, Marvin and Marvin's relatives when Barney showed up. Now that this was over Anancy turned his thoughts to those pesky birds.

A HOME FOR RUFUS

later that week, Anancy was on his way home from paying a visit to Mia, with whom he had spent the greater part of the morning. Midway on his journey, he stopped to rest. On the lower part of the tree, Anancy saw a fat bug caught in a web he had craftily hidden among the thick leaves. Thanking his good luck, he thought, "Ha, I have found my lunch." Preparing to enjoy this unexpected meal, Anancy spotted Brer Rufus, a stout yellow cat with chewed up ears and fur missing from his short stumpy tail. Anancy had often seen Rufus being chased by Sly Fox. Now, here was Rufus sitting on top of a high wall that encircled a large house. Rufus seemed to be gazing rather pensively towards the house, which had once been his home.

As it so happened, Rufus' thoughts were filled with many vexing problems. He couldn't forget the day when his lovely world came crashing down. He had reasoned that it was not his fault; there was this noisy Canary who, when not flying about in his silly golden cage, was forever chirping loudly and disturbing his sleep. When he saw the cage door ajar one morning, how could he pass up the opportunity to get rid of this noisy bird? Rufus, climbed up to open the cage door a little wider and quickly made a grab for the Canary but misjudged its swiftness. The Canary flew by him out into the room and perched on a table amid dainty figurines. In his haste to get his paw out of the cage, Rufus knocked it off the shelf where it was resting and onto the floor with a loud bang. But the loudest crash of all came when Rufus landed on the table with the figurines, which toppled over onto the floor with a tremendous clatter.

Fortunately for Rufus, the table had not fallen on him, but he was covered with bits of china and broken glass. Getting up, he saw the Canary looking down mockingly at him from a high perch, far out of reach and chirping noisily away. The door opened suddenly, and in rushed the cigar-smelling old man who lived there. He angrily grabbed Rufus by the scruff of his neck and Rufus felt himself flying through the open window. Down he dropped into a rose bush full of sharp, evil-looking thorns.

Rufus had quite a job extricating himself from the bush as the thorns clung to his fur and dug into his paws. Poor Rufus spent days nursing his very sore paws and dragging out thorns from his fur. To make matters worse, Rufus was banished from the house. His mistress never again patted or put him on her lap or rocked him gently in her chair while she read her book. But the worst thing for Rufus, was being replaced by two gold fish in a glass bowl. They swam around all day and mocked him whenever he ventured near the window of the room. Rufus thought, with so many fish in the river nearby, why should anyone want to keep two silly looking gold fish in a glass bowl in their home?

A few days later, in a jealous rage, Rufus climbed up a tree near an open window. Jumping onto the ledge, he saw to his delight that it was the room that held the two gold fish in their bowl. The temptation proved too great for him. So, as silently as a mouse, he went up to the glass bowl, and although he hated getting his paws wet, Rufus quickly grabbed a wriggling fish.

The door opened with a bang. Who should appear but the same smelly old man holding the door with one hand, and a long hunting gun with the other. With a roar the man lunged at

Rufus. His heart pounding in terror and fright, Rufus dropped his catch and raced to the open window. He looked back once and saw the man aiming his hunting gun. As Rufus leapt into the trees, he heard a mighty roar and felt as though his tail was on fire. Bounding away, he raced into the woods to a special hiding place to lick his poor wounded tail.

Rufus' troubles, however, were not over yet. Resting on top of the high wall, Rufus was feeling very weary after chasing rabbits all day without any success. And that morning, he awakened to find that a stranger, somewhat like the old man, had moved in during the night and taken over his hiding place. Not only did the stranger seem as if he intended to stay in Rufus' small hut forever, but he had ordered Rufus to go and catch him a rabbit as he felt like having rabbit stew for dinner.

Suddenly, Rufus had an idea. If he could not catch a rabbit, why not a field mouse? It would make a much better stew than some old rabbit anyway. The more Rufus thought of it, the better it seemed. Leaping down from the high wall, Rufus started walking through the woods. Near a group of trees, up popped a field mouse. Crouching silently, Rufus pounced upon the poor unsuspecting mouse, and then headed home.

As Rufus entered the open door of the hut, he saw the intruder stirring a pot on the stove. Looking up and seeing Rufus with what he thought was a rabbit, he gave a big smile showing his large and ugly yellowing teeth. "Ha," he said. "I knew you would not disappoint me." Rufus walked cautiously up to the man and handed over his catch. When the intruder saw that it was only a poor

field mouse, he gave a loud bellow and said, "Making a fool of me, are you?", Grabbing Rufus by his neck, he threw him through the door and yelled, "Get me a rabbit or else don't come back here."

Limping as he walked through the woods, Rufus saw Brer Snake wriggling across his path; and an idea came to him as to how he could get even with that bad-tempered man and maybe get rid of him. And so, Rufus grabbed the snake by its neck and raced to the hut. Silently, he entered the hut and put down the wriggling snake. The intruder had just taken the pot off the stove and on turning around saw the snake. He was terrified of snakes, and seeing one coming towards him, he gave a frightened yelp. He dropped the pot on his left foot and roared again in pain and fright, then rushed through the door of the hut.

All this time, Rufus was hiding under the bed. He laughed quietly as he saw the intruder limping away into the woods.

THE BEDRAGGLED PAIR

Rufus walked wearily towards the river to quench his thirst. Like all cats, he disliked water other than for drinking. He had fallen into the river once while trying to catch a fish in what looked like a shallow pool. To his horror, it had been much deeper. Now quenching his thirst, he was extremely careful.

Rufus had chased rabbits and field mice fruitlessly all day, and he was tired and hungry. He thought that if he waited until it got dark, then he might have better luck. Crouching down on a large stone, he watched the fish as they played and swam lazily around. Feeling drowsy, he stretched out and fell fast asleep, dreaming of a large platter piled high with tastily cooked fish, all ready for his evening meal.

Up in his web, Anancy scowled at Brer Leo, the noisy Bumble Bee, who had just awakened him and then had flew laughingly away through the trees. Following the Bumble Bee with his eyes, Anancy caught sight of Sly Fox creeping silently through the woods, into the field towards the unsuspecting Rufus. "Ha!" Sly Fox said, "I have caught you now, you mangy yellow cat."

Leo, the Bumble Bee who had awakened Anancy, was now buzzing around the sleeping Rufus, who opened his eyes just in time to see Sly Fox leaping through the air at him. Instantly wide awake, Rufus jumped on to a rock in the river and Sly Fox followed. Cornered, Rufus clawed at Sly Fox's eyes and mouth and fled to another rock in the middle of the river. Sly Fox gave chase, but the rock could not hold their combined weight, and it toppled them into the cold river. Rufus thought his world had come to a watery end, but as he surfaced, blinking water from his eyes, he could hardly believe his good luck: A branch floated straight at him! Grabbing hold of it, he paddled downstream, his perch precarious. He wondered how he was ever going to reach the safety of the river bank.

Looking around, he saw Sly Fox swimming towards him and thought that his luck had run out after all. But Sly Fox, seeing his former enemy's plight, had a change of heart and decided to help Rufus. Sly Fox tried pushing

the branch towards the river bank, without success. He called out to Rufus to jump onto his back, which Rufus did. Sly Fox, carrying Rufus, started swimming towards the river bank. Upon reaching the safety of the shore, they both flopped down, drenched, cold and extremely tired. Sly Fox began laughing. Rufus who couldn't see anything laughable about what they had just come through, asked irritably, "What do you find so funny, Sly Fox?"

"Oh, Rufus! You look like a drowned rat, all wet and miserable looking."

Rufus glared at Sly Fox and replied, "You are a sorry sight yourself, with your swollen left eye and that cut on your nose." Then, seeing how funny they both looked, they both started to laugh. An uneasy alliance was formed between the two as they talked about the adventure they just shared.

A little while later, Sly Fox rose from the river bank.

As he turned to leave, he said to Rufus, "My friend, would you like to have dinner with me tonight? I had some good fortune early this morning: I was passing the fowl coop of your former home when suddenly, out of the sky and right into my path fell this plump chicken. Of course, I couldn't leave it lying helplessly there so I took it home. It's all plucked and ready for roasting." Rufus' tummy gave a loud rumble at the thought of food. He agreed readily and followed Sly Fox into the woods.

That night when Anancy and Brer Rabbit met for their nightly talk, Anancy told Brer Rabbit of what had taken place by the river earlier that afternoon between Sly Fox and Rufus. When he got to the part about how they had both looked after their fall into the river, Brer Rabbit laughed so hard that his sides ached. He wished that he, too, could have been there to see the bedraggled pair.

THE CACKLING HEN

Anancy was taking his afternoon nap, as was his custom, when he was rudely awakened by a persistent, noisy buzzing. Opening sleepy eyes, he saw Brer Leo, the bothersome Bumble Bee, hovering about his web. Anancy glared at Leo and cried out in an angry voice, "Get away from here, you miserable creature! You have just disrupted a wonderful dream. Can't you find someone else to go and bother or something to do other than wake me up from my afternoon rest?"

Leo flew onto a twig near Anancy and said, "I thought you might be interested in hearing the big news I heard on one of the stops I made while travelling around today."

Anancy was immediately interested as he loved keeping abreast of what was happening far and near. "Well then, Leo, stop your noisy buzzing and tell me what it is all about," Anancy said grouchily. Leo continued, "Do you remember Marvin, the mouse who once lived in Mia's shack on the other side of the woods?"

"Yes, yes," said Anancy. "Get on with the news and

stop your rambling."

"Well, Anancy, today I learned during one of my stops that poor Marvin is now living in a hen house on a farm. But that's not all. They say that he and Leah, that cackling old hen, have become good friends. Furthermore, they have set up a system with the mean old man with the long gun in hopes to catch poor Sly Fox or stop him from making his nightly visits."

Anancy stretched and said, "Leo, I do not think that they are smart enough to outsmart Sly Fox, especially if Sly Fox and his buddy Rufus team up together. They are sure to find a way around that system."

"Whatever you say, Anancy," Leo buzzed. "If I get more news. I will stop by." And off Leo flew.

Later that evening, Anancy, feeling very disappointed that Brer Rabbit had not come for their usual evening talk, started climbing slowly up his silken thread from the spot on the low branch where he usually awaited Brer Rabbit's coming. Anancy had almost finished his climb when he paused for a hopeful last look below. A rustling in the trees made Anancy look more closely, but it was not Brer Rabbit. It was Marvin the mouse, wandering around. Continuing his climb up the silken thread to his web above, Anancy wondered what could have happened to keep his friend Brer Rabbit away.

Meanwhile, Marvin the mouse was not very happy with his present home. So, on his way to visit friends on the other side of the woods, Marvin decided to take the opportunity to check out the different areas he was passing through. Liking the area he found himself in, Marvin was busily looking around when a sound nearby had him

peering nervously around a tree. To his dismay, he saw
coming through the trees in his direction none other than
his two enemies, Rufus and Sly Fox.

Marvin quickly scampered to safety up Anancy's tree;
he knew that either of the two terrible creatures below
would make a swift meal of him. Peering down through
the branches, Marvin saw, to his further distress, that Sly
Fox and Rufus appeared to be settling down beneath the
very tree in which he was hiding. Rufus with a sigh, curled
up on a bed of soft, dried leaves, and Sly Fox yawned
as he lay down beside him.

"How was your day Rufus?" Sly Fox murmured.

"Well," said Rufus, "today was not one of my lucky days. I only managed to find a few small scraps all day. I did see a mouse earlier on, but the silly mouse disappeared before I had a chance to go after him."

"My luck wasn't much better than yours," murmured Sly Fox sleepily, "but I do wish I could find a way of getting into that hen house without that cackling Leah creating her usual noise and alerting that mean and bad-tempered man with the long gun."

Marvin, curious to know what Sly Fox and Rufus were saying below, lost his balance in the tree and fell heavily upon a sleeping Rufus. With a startled yelp, Rufus jumped high in the air. Then, looking around fearfully, Rufus saw under the tree a horrified Marvin gazing at him with terrified eyes.

Rufus, with an angry leap, pounced upon the hapless Marvin. Seeing the mouse held firmly in Rufus' paws, Sly Fox said, "Lucky you, Rufus, you have your supper dropping from the trees for you. I think I should now go and try my luck over at the hen house and see if a nice fat hen will fall out of the sky for me too."

Marvin, in a frightened and squeaky voice whispered, "Please Sly Fox, save me. Do not let Rufus eat me! I can be of great use to you, Sly Fox, as I live in the same hen house that you are about to visit. I know of a way of getting you inside without Leah making her usual fuss."

Anancy from his web was taking a keen interest in the events that were taking place under his tree. Seeing the danger that poor Marvin was in, he quickly descended on his silken thread to the scene below. He called out, "Hello, Sly Brer Fox. Do not let Rufus hurt Marvin. Only today I heard that Marvin is living in the hen house just like he said. And furthermore, from what that nosy, noisy Bumble Bee Leo told me, I am sure Marvin can get you in and out of the hen house without Leah making a noise."

Sly Fox, his interest aroused said, "Well, Marvin, how can you make this happen?" Marvin, feeling a little less scared, said in a firmer voice, "Leah and I have become good friends, especially after I told her a few days ago that I overheard the miserable old man telling someone that she was almost too old for laying and although she might be a bit tough, if cooked properly, she still could be eaten. I am sure she will keep quiet if I ask her not to cackle tonight. There is only one small problem. After tonight, you and Rufus will have to find a new home for Leah, as that bad-tempered old man will surely wring poor Leah's neck for not alerting him with her cackling."

"Marvin," Anancy said, "I also heard of this great system that you, Leah and the old man have set up to catch Sly Fox. What is it all about?"

"Well," said Marvin, taking Anancy's bait, "the way

the system works is this: I act as the lookout for Sly Fox, and as soon as I spot you, I give a signal to Leah who then immediately starts her cackling. This will alert the man with the long gun, who will hide near the hen house and await Sly Fox's arrival. But you will never arrive."

Late that night, after repeated noisy cackling by Leah and still no sign of Sly Fox, the old man with the gun got tired of waiting in the damp and cold night air. With an angry look at Leah for setting off those false alarms, he stormed away from the hen house, telling Leah that in the morning he would deal with her severely.

As soon as the old man closed his door, Sly Fox came out of the hiding place that Marvin had led him to earlier. Sly Fox silently entered the hen house where the young and plucked chickens were kept before being sent off to the different markets that the farm supplied each day. Sly Fox called to Rufus who had been waiting in a tree nearby, and they both filled their sacks with as many of the freshly plucked chickens as they could hold. Slinging the sacks over their shoulders, off they went with happy smiles on their faces, and also in great anticipation of the lovely feast they would enjoy after they reached home. Following closely behind Sly Fox and Rufus were Leah and Marvin, going along with their newly made friends to their new home in the woods.

AN IMPROBABLE
FOURSOME

Some months later Anancy and Brer Rabbit, along with Mia, who had joined them in their nightly get-together, were sitting on an old tree-trunk under Anancy's tree. Ever since Barney the owl had scared off Marvin the mouse, Mia lived by herself in the old shack on the other side of the woods. Earlier that day, she had come over to visit with Anancy. Seeing that she was lonely, Anancy had asked her to stay on.

All three friends were enjoying a quiet chat, exchanging their views on the different events in the woods and on what was happening in their own lives. Anancy talked of his usual troubles with his pesky birds; they had now taken over most of his tree and their noisy chattering was getting on his nerves. Brer Rabbit complained that someone or something was rooting up and destroying nearly all of his vegetables again; could Anancy come up with another way to help him find and get rid of the culprit? Mia remarked that since Marvin's departure, her shack seemed a bit too quiet. She had not minded Marvin's presence; it was his noisy relatives and friends she objected to.

During a lull in their conversation, the three friends became aware of Sly Brer Fox coming through the trees towards them. Anancy voiced what they were all thinking: "I wonder if he is going to be his miserable self and play his usual tricks on us?"

Sly Fox seeing his former enemies' uneasiness, called out to them in a loud and cheerful voice: "Hello there, good friends! This must be my lucky night. I really wanted to see each of you sometime soon. Now finding you all together tonight is simply perfect!"

As Sly Fox spoke his other three friends—Rufus the cat, Marvin the mouse and Leah, the hen, joined him. Mia's eyes nearly popped out of her head, as she had not known that a friendship had been formed by the most unlikely looking foursome now settling themselves under Anancy's tree.

"Well," Anancy said, "what has brought you all here tonight? Speak up, Sly Fox, as it seems that you are the leader of the group!"

"Anancy," Sly Fox replied, "we four are badly in need of a new home. We all wish to remain together, but the weather is about to change and three of my friends here will not be able to withstand the cold living outdoors."

"I'm sorry, Sly Fox," Anancy said, "this tree of mine would not be a suitable place for any of you."

"Sly Fox," Brer Rabbit said, "my house is largely underground, and you and Rufus would find my quarters a bit confining."

They all turned and looked at Mia who had kept quiet as they talked. Now, in a resigned voice, she said. "I+

is true that I have this shack, and lately I have been feeling a bit lonely. But, four of you! That's more than I had bargained for. Anyway, come over and we will find out if we can all live comfortably in the shack during the winter months. I must warn you that the shack must be kept clean and tidy at all times."

With peals of happy laughter, the unlikely foursome did a hop and a jig around Anancy, Brer Rabbit and Mia. Then, with smiles on their faces, they thanked Mia profusely, promising to pay her a visit soon, and off they went into the woods.

After Sly Fox and his three friends departed, Mia said, "I really had no choice but to take them into my house, but what have I got myself into?" Both Brer Rabbit and Anancy tried to reassure her. "It was a very good deed you have just done," said Anancy, "as they will be needing the shack when the weather changes. Also, you once said that Marvin on his own was on the quiet side, and Leah has no cause to cackle now. Rufus with a full belly will sleep forever if he is allowed. That leaves Sly Fox, and even he seems to have changed from being a miserable and troublesome creature. We shall see if he can keep up his new self, especially since he has assumed leadership of the pack."

The three friends chatted for a while longer and then Brer Rabbit and Mia said their goodbyes and left. Anancy, alone now and settling down in the web for the night, could not stop thinking of Mia and the houseful she would soon have in her shack. He reasoned and was comforted that Mia would be less lonely and her life would certainly become more interesting.

A few days later, the unlikely foursome—fox, cat, mouse and hen—visited Mia as promised, to look over her shack. Mia descended from her web in the ceiling to greet her visitors. After much discussion about how they would all fit in the shack without bothering each other, they each chose a corner.

During the discussion and the working out of the plan, Leah was having second thoughts about the new living arrangements. She wondered how Sly Fox would react to her close presence. When the food supply got short during the winter months, wouldn't she be too much of a temptation for his hungry belly to withstand? She began to think that the wisest course for her would be to quietly seek somewhere else to live and not tempt fate in the form of Sly Fox. There was a farm with a large hen house a long distance away from here. She would go there, and, as her laying days were not quite over, she would be safe for some time yet.

Meanwhile Marvin the mouse was having the same doubts, especially where Rufus the cat was concerned. His grandchildren were very noisy and quarrelsome, but right now their home on the other side of the woods seemed a much safer place than the set up here promised to be. On their way home, Marvin and Leah walked slowly together while Rufus and Sly Fox raced ahead.

Leah looked at Marvin and murmured, "I had a bad feeling back there about living in such a confined space with Sly Fox during the long winter months, especially if our food gets scarce. What do you think of the arrangement?"

Marvin, not at all surprised by Leah's remarks, confided, "I also had that strange feeling inside of me about living that close to Rufus. I think Rufus might just take a keener interest in me, too, if our food supplies run out." With their minds full of the dangers they might expect in the near future, they both decided to keep a close watch on Rufus' and Sly Fox's movements.

A few days later, they all moved into Mia's old shack. Winter had hardly set in when food started to become scarce. Late one night, Marvin, a light sleeper, heard sounds coming from Sly Fox's corner. After listening for a while, he went across to Leah, who was also awake. The two crept nearer to Sly Fox, who was muttering in his sleep, going on about food shortages and being snowbound by storms. Leah and Marvin's fears were greatly aroused when, smiling widely and smacking his chops, Sly Fox muttered Leah's name, then Marvin's, and reflected on how handy it was having such a meal in reserve!

Mia, who had quietly joined the two, saw the distress on their faces and told them of a safe place where they could stay for a while. Thanking her for being such a helpful friend, they quickly packed their bags and silently slipped through the door into the night. After they left, Mia climbed back up to her web, musing that Sly Fox would have to look for winter food elsewhere. She glanced down at Rufus snoring softly in his corner of the shack and thought that perhaps he should soon think about leaving Sly Fox too.

RUFUS' REVENGE

The winter stretched on.

Anancy, during one of his many outings, found himself in a beautiful shady tree. He thought it had great possibilities for a future home - in the event that he wanted to leave his present one. He decided to spend a couple of days exploring its branches. Looking down from his high perch, he saw Rufus approaching his tree. His curiosity was immediately aroused as he saw Sly Fox not too far behind, creeping silently on his belly so as not to attract attention.

Anancy watched as Rufus climbed up the tree, which grew beside a big house that he wanted to investigate. The tree's many branches and thick leaves made a perfect hiding place, yet they offered an excellent view into the kitchen of the house. As Rufus scampered to his chosen branch, Sly Fox seized the opportunity to dash unseen into the bushes below the open window.

Rufus, looking into the kitchen from his vantage point, intently watched the lady of the house, Mrs. Tomasina. She was a big gray haired woman standing beside a stove frying a big pan of fish. Earlier that day, Rufus had observed her buying the fish in the market. He had carefully worked out a way of helping himself to a portion of it. In anticipation of a mouthwatering feast, he now patiently studied the old lady as she placed one piece after the other of nicely fried fish on a large platter.

After putting the last morsel on the platter, now piled high with deliciously cooked fish, she left the kitchen, carefully closing the door behind her. The aroma of freshly fried fish coming through the window made Rufus' tummy rumble, reminding him that he had not eaten all day. Rufus decided that the time had come to put his plan into action. Swiftly, he leapt on to the window sill and into the kitchen with his bag, which he had brought along for the special purpose of taking home his lovely dinner.

He rapidly filled his bag and leaping back onto the

window sill, carefully lowered his heavy bag into the bushes growing under the window. Hearing a sound behind the closed door, he hurriedly jumped into the tree, then scurried down to collect his catch. Arriving at the spot in the bushes where he thought he had left the bag, Rufus was surprised and mystified to find it gone! Searching furiously and still with no sign of the bag, he became hopping mad. He was now sure that someone had stolen his much anticipated meal.

Anancy meanwhile, had been observing Rufus, and Sly Fox—observing the unfolding events. He watched a hungry and crestfallen Rufus leave for home. Rufus, on arriving at the shack he shared with Sly Fox and Mia, found his wily friend Brer Fox fast asleep and snoring in his corner; knowing that Sly Fox was usually wide awake and eagerly awaiting his return, he became immediately suspicious, especially as Sly Fox always wanted half of whatever it was Rufus brought home. He could not help wondering if that miserable Sly Fox had followed him and stolen his bag of fish; "He'll pay dearly," Rufus muttered to himself as, stomach growling, he settled down to a restless night.

Next morning, Sly Brer Fox opened his sleepy eyes and yawned as he looked across at Rufus. Seeing that he was wide awake, Sly Fox said craftily: "Yesterday, I was so tired from chasing rabbits all day without much success. I found only small portions along the way. After reaching home, I fell asleep immediately. I never even heard when you got in. What about your day? More successful than mine?"

Rufus, realizing by Sly Fox's manner that he was the thieving rascal, could barely control his anger. But he answered calmly, as if all was well between them. "My day could have been better," he said. "Like you, friend, I did manage to find a few bits and pieces to eat during the day." Despite his bravado, Rufus was still very hungry and tired from a restless night. He thought that maybe if he returned to the old lady's house there might yet be a few fish left over in the kitchen.

Later that morning, Anancy, who had spent the night in his new tree, saw Rufus making his way silently on to the branch that overlooked the open kitchen window. Once again, there was Sly Fox creeping quietly below, watching as Rufus climbed up the tree, then darting into the bushes under the window. Looking inside, Rufus saw the old lady talking to the gardener. He could hear them discussing a trap to catch the thief who had stolen most of her fish the previous day. He watched as she placed a batch of

fried fish by the window. Turning back to the stove, she finished frying a new batch which she placed in a cupboard. With a quick look around the kitchen they left the room.

Anancy, suspecting what Rufus might be up to, quickly descended on his silken thread to join a startled Rufus. He pointed down at Sly Brer Fox hiding in the bushes below the open window. In a whisper, Rufus told Anancy about the discussion he had just overheard between the old lady and the gardener. He explained to Anancy that he had decided to use their trap to snare Sly Fox. Their plan was a much better one than he had thought of himself.

Leaping onto the open window, then into the kitchen, Rufus carefully filled his first bag with the fish set out specially for the thief. He lowered it down into the bushes where a patient Sly Fox awaited its arrival. Peeping over the window sill, Rufus saw Sly Fox as he snatched up the bag and raced away laughing to himself. When he was out of sight, Rufus filled the other bag with the batch of fish from the cupboard. Then, leaping back into the tree with his precious cargo, he made his way carefully down. Checking that no one was around, he raced to an abandoned hut he had carefully scouted out some time before. Putting down his bag, he rested for a while, then settled down to enjoy a lovely dinner of fried fish.

Later, when he returned to Mia's shack, Rufus saw Sly Fox doubled up in pain and groaning loudly. Knowing quite well that the fish Sly Fox had just eaten was cooked in mixture that would cause the mouth to burn unbearably and the belly to ache in a terrible way, Rufus now asked innocently, "Sly Fox, what's wrong? Are you ill?"

Sly Fox looked up with pain and anger in his eyes and snarled at Rufus. He was quite sure that Rufus had something to do with his present suffering, or at least knew the cause. Much later, Anancy stopped by to find out how Sly Fox had fared. He and Rufus had a hearty laugh at Sly Fox's expense.

ANANCY GOES FISHING

Anancy felt tired and decided to rest for a while from the never-ending mending of his web on the topmost branch of his favorite tree. As he looked tiredly towards the open field bordering the woods and the river beyond it, he saw Brer Rabbit pop out from the trees.

Anancy watched as Brer Rabbit hopped through the open field heading for the river which rippled over the stones and around a large rock. Behind the rock, a pool lapped gently, deep enough for the unwary fish to think they were safe from the anglers further up stream. The fish were also quite unaware that this was Brer Rabbit's favorite fishing hole. As Brer Rabbit set about getting his rod, reel, and flies ready to catch his afternoon meal, Anancy saw Sly Fox creeping on his belly through the trees, silent as a mouse, trying hard not to attract Brer Rabbit's attention.

Sly Fox smacked his lips in silent anticipation and patiently waited. Brer Rabbit laughed as he hooked his first catch, a large gleaming fish. He unhooked it carefully, hopped to his basket sitting on a fallen log nearby and

lovingly placed the fish inside. Then, Brer Rabbit turned back to the river with his reel, his mind intent on a particularly huge fish that had given him the slip all too often. At last he hooked him, and went, whistling and jigging to deposit him in his basket. But when he lifted the lid to put in his latest catch, lo and behold, his basket was empty! Brer Rabbit looked all around the open field but no one was in sight. Mystified, he hopped slowly back to the woods.

Anancy, who had seen the whole thing, swiftly slid down his silken thread and called out to Brer Rabbit. "Brer Rabbit, my friend," he said. "I was resting after a particularly hard day of mending my web, which was destroyed by the wind and rain and by those pesky birds that have just made their nests in my tree, when who should I see creeping through the woods but Sly Fox. He waited until you had settled down on that large rock. Then, he hid himself behind the very large rock on which you had rested your basket."

The two friends agreed that they would once again have to put their heads together to deal once and for all with Sly Fox. They thought of many different ruses, but nothing ideal came to mind. Finally, Brer Rabbit said to Anancy, "At least we have one fish that we can share tonight, and by tomorrow when we meet again, something may occur to us."

Next morning, Anancy called to Brer Rabbit as he was on his way to his garden patch. "Brer Rabbit," he said, "I have an idea of how we can finally outsmart Sly Fox."

Two days later, Brer Rabbit hopped back to his favorite fishing hole near the large rock. This time he set his basket on a log near to a large tree that had branches spreading out over the river. Brer Rabbit hummed as he brought in his first catch, which was even bigger than the previous one. Smiling, Brer Rabbit placed it in his basket, then

picked up his pole and hopped back to the pool. Anancy watched as Sly Fox crept out of the woods on his belly and stealthily approached the basket. Sly Fox opened the basket and grabbed the fish between his large chops. A sudden sound startled him and, as he turned quickly around, he stepped on a sharp object that went right through his right front paw. He howled in pain as he tried to get the evil-looking silver hook from his paw.

Suddenly, there was a sharp tug and Sly Fox felt himself being pulled by his very sore paw toward the nearby tree. Brer Rabbit appeared from the other side of the tree with a fishing pole in his hand. He wrapped the line around the tree and Sly Fox was neatly caught. Anancy soon appeared to admire Brer Rabbit's handiwork. Roaring with pain and anger at being caught and strung up, Sly Fox begged and pleaded with Brer Rabbit and Anancy to free him, promising that he would do anything they wanted of him, and that he would never steal Brer Rabbit's fish or his turnips and carrots again.

Brer Rabbit and Anancy conferred for a few minutes, and then Brer Rabbit said: "First, Sly Fox, you must come early in the morning for a month and weed my garden patch. Second, at mid-morning of the month you will stop and gather fire wood and bring it to my hole. Third, you will catch and cook my evening meal of fish for the whole month."

Sly Fox having no choice agreed to all of these terms, but as he slunk off into the woods he vowed that he would never rest until he had got his revenge on both Brer Rabbit and his clever friend, Anancy.

And so, until today, Brer Fox is still trying to get even with Anancy.